Stanley Stone Rocks!

Karen McCombie

Illustrated by
Beatriz Castro

OXFORD

OXFORD

UNIVERSITY PRESS

Great Clarendon Street, Oxford, OX2 6DP,
United Kingdom

Oxford University Press is a department of the University of Oxford.
It furthers the University's objective of excellence in research, scholarship,
and education by publishing worldwide. Oxford is a registered trade mark of
Oxford University Press in the UK and in certain other countries

British Library Cataloguing in Publication Data
Data available

978-0-19-837732-0

1 3 5 7 9 10 8 6 4 2

Paper used in the production of this book is a natural, recyclable product
made from wood grown in sustainable forests. The manufacturing process
conforms to the environmental regulations of the country of origin.

Printed in China by Leo Paper Products Ltd.

Acknowledgements
Inside cover notes written by Gill Howell
Author photograph by Louise Millar

Contents

1   Too New   5

2   The Strange Stone   14

3   How to Feel Cheerful   20

4   Badda-boom!   26

5   The Bring-Your-Pet-to-
    School Show!   32

6   Not So Fast!   38

7   A REAL Reward   45

About the author   48

Chapter 1
Too New

Frank sighed.

Everything was just too new. He sat on his bed in his new school uniform and stared around at his new bedroom, with its blank walls and empty shelves. It just didn't feel right. Frank hadn't yet unpacked all his toys and books and bits and bobs. But he knew that even after he had, the room would *still* feel too icky and new.

Frank's bedroom

"Frank! Nancy! Breakfast!" he heard
Dad call.

Sighing another sigh, Frank got up
and walked through to the new kitchen.

It was so different from the *old* kitchen in the *old* flat in the town they used to live in.

The *old* kitchen was cosy and colourful and smelled of crumpets in the morning. The *new* one was shiny and sheeny and smelled of fresh paint. At least their own, familiar pine table and chairs were in there.

Sadly, so was Frank's big sister Nancy.

She made a rude face at Frank. Then she smiled as soon as Dad turned around with a big box of cereal in his hand.

"So, it's your first day at Beechwood School. Looking forward to it?" Dad asked, smiling.

"Yes! Can't wait!" said Nancy.

Frank said nothing, but he felt all grumbly inside. It was all right for Nancy. She liked new things. She was a chatty, bubbly, bouncy sort of person. She could make lots of friends quicker than Frank could blow his nose.

Frank was the opposite. He liked it when things stayed the same. He was a quiet, shy, wibbly-wobbly sort of person. He only had one-and-a-half friends at his old school. (Yusuf was fine, but Charlie could be a real pest – Frank still hadn't forgiven him for scribbling all over his best drawing of a robot.)

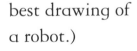

"Feeling OK, Frank?" asked Dad,
giving Frank a little pat on the shoulder.
"Not really," mumbled Frank.
"Oh, dear ..." said Dad, frowning.
"Anything I can do to make it better?"

A little glow of hope lit up inside
Frank. There *was* something that Dad
could do. Something that might stop
him feeling so lonely in his new world.

"Well, I was just wondering … could
I have a pet?" Frank asked Dad.

"Sorry, Frank," Dad answered. "There
are no pets allowed in these flats."

Frank was pretty sure that meant
BIG pets, like cats and dogs and ponies
and goats and stuff. Frank wasn't
thinking of one of those. He'd be happy
with something small,
fuzzy and cuddly.

"How about a hamster?" Frank asked.

"No," Dad said more firmly.

Dad didn't notice, but Nancy was making a face at Frank again.

Frank wished he was bad and brave enough to flick a spoonful of soggy cereal at his sister. But he wasn't good at being bad or brave, just as he wasn't good at new and different things.

"Now hurry up and eat your breakfast," Dad said cheerfully. "It's nearly time for school!"

Frank knew the time. It was time to have a big, fat, squashy *sulk* ...

Chapter 2
The Strange Stone

Phew!

It was the end of Frank and Nancy's first day at Beechwood School. Nancy was *supposed* to be walking home with Frank through the park. But instead, she was way ahead of him, giggling with some new friends.

Frank didn't have any new friends yet. He just had a headache. Starting at a new school meant so much thinking. Like trying to remember the teacher's name and worrying about where the toilets were.

Today, Frank had lots of tiring feelings too. Feelings like being scared, lonely and confused.

Still, there *had* been some OK bits. His new teacher (Miss Patel) had a nice smile.

A girl with red hair showed him her best cartwheel.

And there was yummy toffee pudding for school dinner.

But even so, Frank wasn't happy. He wished everything was just like it used to be. Feeling grumpy, he kicked at a stone on the path. It skittered up ahead.

He kicked it again.

It skittered some more. One more kick, and this time the stone ended up tumbling into the grass. Frank walked over, getting ready to whack it back on to the path with the toe of his school shoe. Then something made him stop. He stared down at the stone.

How strange! It wasn't properly round. It was an odd shape. Knobbly. A bit like a knobbly, hairless *hamster*, if you looked at it funny, which Frank was doing right now.

Bending, Frank scooped up the stone, slipped it in his pocket, and started to walk faster. His mind was going faster too. That was because Frank was thinking of the stick-on googly eyes in the craft box at home.

With the help of those, he'd soon have his own pet after all!

Chapter 3
How to Feel Cheerful

The next morning, Nancy stopped so
quickly outside the school gate that
Frank bumped into her. Nancy scowled
down at her little brother. Actually,
she scowled more at what Frank
was holding.

"Please don't tell me you're taking
that thing into school!" said Nancy.

"It's not a THING!" said Frank. "It's
STANLEY. Stanley Stone."

Frank stroked the rock. With the googly eyes on, it looked ever so cute and funny.

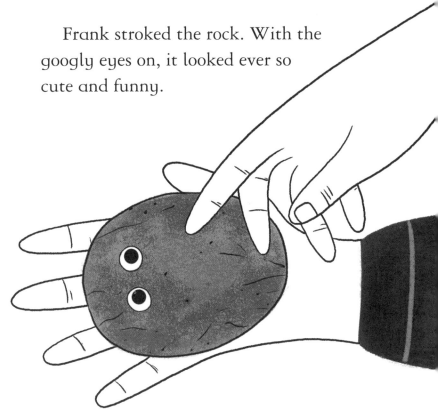

Frank had wanted a hamster or gerbil or goldfish to cuddle, but now that he had Stanley Stone he forgot about all of those.

"Everyone will think you're totally mad," said Nancy.

"I don't know *everyone* here, so I don't care," Frank said cheerfully.

It was nice to feel cheerful; Frank had almost forgotten how. He'd been *un*-cheerful for such a long time. Ever since Dad told them they were moving, in fact.

But now here was Stanley Stone, and Frank was not alone. If he had no one to play with today, he could play with Stanley Stone. If he forgot someone's name or the way to the toilet, he would cuddle Stanley Stone till he could remember. Today would be a good day!

Frank and Nancy both heard the laughing at the same time. It was a mean sort of laughing. It was coming from a big boy who was pointing at Frank's pet as if it was silly and stupid.

Inside, Frank knew that the big boy was probably silly and stupid. But the meanness still left Frank with a flippy-floppy feeling in his tummy that he didn't much like.

Then an unexpected thing happened. Nancy put her arm around Frank and gave him a squeeze.

"Got a problem?" she snapped at the big boy.

"Er, no," said the big boy, who was now looking a teensy bit scared. Frank suddenly felt very glad he had a sister who could be slightly fierce.

"Good!" Nancy smiled brightly. "Let's go, Frank."

"*And* Stanley," Frank reminded her.

"OK, *and* Stanley," Nancy added as they walked towards the school entrance.

Frank's tummy flip-flops instantly turned into flitter-flutters of happiness.

Chapter 4
Badda-boom!

So far, Frank's second day at school had been quite surprising. He'd remembered nearly everyone's name *and* where the toilet was. Boys and girls in class kept talking to him. He felt a whole lot less shy. And it was all because of Stanley Stone!

Now it was afternoon break and Frank was having the best fun.

"Can I hold him again?" asked the red-haired girl who was good at cartwheels.

"OK, but don't drop him!" said Frank, carefully passing Stanley Stone over to her.

The red-haired girl was called Elsie. She stroked Stanley Stone very gently and whispered, "Who's a good boy?" to him.

Elsie and Frank were in the middle of a big huddle of children, who all wanted a turn holding Stanley. Frank beamed when he heard what people were saying.

I want one!

Aw! It's so cute!

That new boy is so lucky!

Even Miss Patel had gone a bit mushy over Stanley and *ooh*-ed when she'd first seen him this morning. But now Frank heard a different, deep, grown-up sort of voice.

"Well, what's going on here?" it asked.

Frank looked up and saw the voice belonged to Mr Donald, the head teacher. Frank knew who Mr Donald was. He'd talked at assembly yesterday morning but Frank couldn't remember much of what he said. That's because yesterday was a long time ago. A time when Frank had felt scared and sad.

But today was brand new and good. So Frank smiled shyly at Mr Donald and tried to talk too, though that was a little harder. Luckily, Elsie wasn't shy and explained for him.

"Look, Mr Donald!" she said, holding up Stanley Stone for the head teacher to see. "This is Frank and this is his pet."

"Well, nice to meet you, Frank,"
said Mr Donald. "And nice to meet …
um …"

"Stanley Stone," said Frank, finding
his voice at last.

"Would you like to hold him, Mr
Donald?" asked Elsie.

"Yes! Yes, I would!" said Mr Donald,
reaching out his big hands. "This is a
very fine pet indeed, Frank. In fact, I'd
say Stanley Stone rocks!"

Yesterday, Frank's heart felt soggy
and sad and bruised. But now his heart
was badda-booming with pride and joy!

Chapter 5
The Bring-Your-Pet-to-School Show!

Frank and Stanley Stone had been at Beechwood School for three whole weeks now, which was practically forever.

Actually, when Frank tried to remember his old school and old home in the old town, his memory went all fuzzy around the edges. He was having way too much fun with Stanley Stone, Elsie and everyone else in class. And today was going to be the best fun yet, because there was a Bring-Your-Pet-to-School Show! Right now the school hall was stuffed with boys, girls and grown-ups, as well as mewing, barking, squeaking and snuffling animals.

Two judges (Mr Donald and the lady who owned the local dog grooming shop) were wandering around, inspecting all of the animals. At the far end of the hall was a table. It was covered in colourful, silky, very special-looking rosettes that said things like 'Smartest Pet', 'Prettiest Pet' and 'Most Talented Pet'.

"Are you excited, Frank?" Elsie asked. Elsie was cuddling her squishy rabbit called Nibbles, who was nibbling at Elsie's hair, just in case it might taste nice.

"Yes, I'm excited," said Frank, looking around at all the dogs on leads and gerbils in cages and hamsters in balls. Everyone else's pets looked fun or sweet. But none were as special or interesting as Stanley Stone. Fingers crossed Mr Donald and the dog grooming lady would think so too!

"Hey, the judges are coming!" Frank heard his sister Nancy whisper in his ear.

Eek! Frank gazed down at Stanley Stone all cupped and cosy in his hand and whispered, "Good luck!" Stanley Stone looked back up at Frank with his googly eyes and seemed very excited too.

"Hurrumph!"

At that snorty sound, Frank glanced up and saw the dog grooming lady snatch up Stanley Stone.

"Is this a joke?" she said crossly.

"Er, no. This is my pet," Frank answered in a small and shaky voice. The dog grooming lady stared hard at Frank as she handed Stanley Stone back to him.

"Young man," she barked, "this is NOT an actual animal, is it? So please take your rock away and sit down."

Sharp, stingy tears prickled in Frank's eyes. He hadn't known words could hurt. It felt like a slap. Holding poor Stanley Stone tight, Frank ran.

Chapter 6
Not So Fast!

Dad and Nancy caught up with Frank in the hallway and wrapped him up in double hugs. Hiding inside their arms, Frank sniffled and snuffled and felt very small indeed.

"What a rude person!" he heard Dad mutter about the dog grooming lady.

"What a rude, NO-FUN person!" he heard Nancy grumble, which made Frank nearly, but not quite, smile.

Then Frank heard another voice. A voice that sounded smiley.

"Frank!" Elsie called out. "Can you come back into the hall? Please?"

"What do you think, Frank?" said Dad, as he and Nancy loosened their hugs and stared at him. Frank didn't say anything. He didn't think he wanted to go back into the hall.

"Oh, come on," said Elsie. "It's something good. Promise!"

Frank felt Elsie slip her hand into his. In his other hand was Stanley, who looked a bit curious, as if he wanted to know what was going on. So Frank let Elsie lead him back into the hall, where a crowd was gathered around the table with the prize rosettes.

And there was the dog grooming lady, looking stunned. Frank wondered why, and hurried over for a closer look.

Ah, NOW he understood!

The dog grooming lady was stunned because Frank's schoolmates were showing her their *own* stone pets.

Hey, it wasn't only Frank who'd found new friends in the last few weeks; Stanley Stone had too!

Everyone had been sticking their own googly eyes on to random stones that they'd found. Even Mr Donald had one, with glasses drawn on with a black felt pen.

"Ah, Frank!" Mr Donald boomed as soon as he spotted him. "Sorry, it was just a little misunderstanding back there."

"Yes," added Miss Patel, who was holding something frilly and round, and made of coloured tissue paper and wet glue. "And this is for you – and Stanley Stone, of course!"

Frank took the frilly something from his teacher. It had a circle of white card in the middle, and in Miss Patel's best writing it said: 'Pet That Rocks!'

Wow! Stanley Stone had WON a prize!

Pet
That
Rocks!

"Wow! Pretty special, huh?" said
Elsie, holding Nibbles back so he couldn't
munch Stanley's extra-special rosette.

But Frank – who was hip-hopping
with happiness – could hardly hear his
friend, thanks to all the cheering (and
barking and howling) in the hall …

Chapter 7
A REAL Reward

Half an hour later, the Bring-Your-Pet-to-School Show was over, and it was Take-Your-Pets-Back-Home time.

As they strolled through the park where Frank had first met Stanley Stone, Dad spoke.

"Well done, son," he said. "I'm so proud of the way you've settled into our new life here."

Frank smiled to himself and hugged Stanley Stone to his chest.

"And I was thinking," Dad carried on. "As a reward, how about we get you a REAL hamster?"

"No way!" Frank told Dad, putting his hands over Stanley Stone's ears, quick as a blink.

"Oh. Sorry," said Dad, realizing he'd said the wrong thing.

"But you know, Dad could *still* get you a present," Nancy said with a grin. "How about a proper cage for Stanley Stone?"

"With a tunnel and exercise wheel?" Frank asked, hopefully.

"Really? *That's* what you want?" Dad frowned down at him.

"Of course," said Frank. "Only the best for the best pet *ever*."

"OK, a cage with a tunnel and exercise wheel!" Dad laughed.

And together they ALL laughed. Even Stanley Stone.

Sort of!

About the author

Growing up, I *longed* for a pet cat. But that wasn't allowed in the flat my family lived in. Sounds familiar? Well, I might have used this as inspiration for the tale of Frank and Stanley Stone, but I definitely didn't have a pet rock myself!

What I finally ended up with was a goldfish, whose name I couldn't decide on. That was until my mum took a new school shirt out of its packet and a sticky label from it fluttered down and stuck to the side of the goldfish tank. The sticky label read '100% Cotton'. It was perfect! My fish lived happily ever after, without realizing what a stupid name it had.